E
B

Burningham, John.
    Where's Julius? / John Burningham. --
New York : Crown Publishers, c1986.
    [32] p. : col. ill. ; 31 cm.
    ISBN 0-517-56476-9 : $9.95

W35

AUG 1987

1. Imagination--Fiction. 2. Play--
Fiction. I. Title

3

MiMtcM 30 JUL 87   13762144   EYBAme   86-13524

Where's Julius?

JOHN BURNINGHAM

CROWN PUBLISHERS, INC.
NEW YORK

Among other books by John Burningham

Granpa
John Burningham's ABC
John Burningham's 123
John Burningham's Colors
John Burningham's Opposites

Copyright © 1986 by John Burningham

Published in the United States by Crown Publishers, Inc.,
225 Park Avenue South, New York, New York 10003.

Published in Great Britain by Jonathan Cape, Ltd.,
32 Bedford Square, London WC1

CROWN is a trademark of Crown Publishers, Inc.

Manufactured in Italy

Library of Congress Cataloging-in-Publication Data
Burningham, John. Where's Julius? Summary: Julius uses his
bold imagination while he plays to enjoy fabulous escapades,
shooting South American rapids and riding camels up
pyramids. [1. Imagination—Fiction. 2. Play—Fiction] I. Title.
PZ7.B936Wh   1986   [E]   86-13524

ISBN 0-517-56476-9   ISBN 0-517-56511-0 (lib. bdg.)

10 9 8 7 6 5 4 3 2 1

First Edition

"For breakfast," said Mrs. Troutbeck, "we have scrambled eggs with mushrooms, cornflakes and some orange juice, which I have unfrozen.

"Where's Julius?"

Mr. Troutbeck called their son Julius and they all sat down to breakfast.

"For lunch today we are having sardines on toast, a roll and butter, tomatoes and nothing for dessert.

"Where's Julius?"

"Julius says he cannot have lunch with us today because he has made a little home in the other room with three chairs, the old curtains and the broom."

So Mr. Troutbeck took the tray with the sardines
on toast, a roll and butter, tomato and
no dessert to the other room where Julius had
made his little home out of three chairs, the old
curtains and the broom.

"I've got the lamb casserole for supper out of the oven and the potatoes in their jackets and broccoli with butter on top and for a treat there is cranberry crunch.

"Where's Julius?"

"Julius says he cannot have supper with us just at
the moment because he is digging a hole in order to
get to the other side of the world."

So Mrs. Troutbeck took the lamb casserole, the
potatoes in their jackets and broccoli with butter
on top and the cranberry crunch for a treat to
where Julius was digging his hole.

"For breakfast there is sausage, bacon and eggs, toast and marmalade and also a glass of Three-Flavor Fruit Juice.

"Where's Julius?"

"Julius says he cannot have breakfast with us today because he is riding a camel to the top of the tomb of Neffatuteum which is a pyramid near the Nile in Egypt."

So Mr. Troutbeck took the tray with the sausage, bacon and egg, toast and marmalade and the glass of Three-Flavor Fruit Juice—and another for the camel—to Egypt where Julius was riding to the top of the pyramid.

"For lunch there is cheese salad with celery and tomato and an orange for dessert if you want it.

"Where's Julius?"

"Julius says he cannot have lunch with us just at the moment because he is cooling the hippopotamuses in the Lombo Bombo River in Central Africa, with buckets of muddy water."

So Mr. Troutbeck took the tray with the cheese salad with celery and tomato and the orange for dessert to Africa where Julius was pouring buckets of muddy water on the hippopotamuses, to keep them cool.

"Here are the grilled chops for supper. There are baby carrots, garden peas and mashed potato to go with them, and an apple crumble for dessert.

"Where's Julius?"

"Julius says he can't have supper with us just at the moment because he is throwing snowballs at the wolves from a sleigh in which he is crossing the frozen wastes of Novosti Krosky which lies somewhere in Russia where the winters are long."

So Mrs. Troutbeck took the tray with the chop, the baby carrots, garden peas and mashed potato and the apple crumble for dessert to Novosti Krosky which lies somewhere in Russia where Julius was throwing snowballs at the wolves.

"For breakfast we are having boiled eggs, toast and marmalade and the tropical fruit juice that you wanted.

"Where's Julius?"

"Julius says he cannot have breakfast with us just at the moment because he is watching the sunrise from the top of the Changa Benang mountains somewhere near Tibet."

So Mr. Troutbeck
took the tray with
the boiled egg,
toast and marmalade
and the tropical
fruit juice
to the top of the
Changa Benang
mountains
somewhere near Tibet,
where Julius was
watching the sunrise.

"For lunch we are having spaghetti bolognese with lettuce and cucumber. For dessert there is fruit flan.

"Where's Julius?"

"Julius says he can't have lunch with us at the moment because he is on a raft which he has made from pieces of wood and old oil drums and he is about to shoot the rapids on the Chico Neeko River somewhere in Peru in South America."

So Mrs. Troutbeck took the tray with the spaghetti bolognese, the lettuce and cucumber and the fruit flan to the Chico Neeko River in South America where Julius was about to shoot the rapids on his raft.

"For supper today there is Mulligan stew,
and tapioca pudding for afterward.

"Is Julius building a home out of old curtains,
chairs and the broom?

Digging a hole to get to the other side of the world?

Riding a camel up a pyramid?

Cooling the hippos that stand in the
Lombo Bombo River?

Throwing snowballs at wolves in Novosti Krosky
where the winters are long?

Is he climbing the Changa Benang mountains,
or shooting the rapids on the Chico Neeko River
in South America?

Perhaps he is helping the young owls to learn
to fly in the trees at the end of the road
or tucking the polar bears in their beds
somewhere in Antarctica?"

"Betty," said Mr. Troutbeck, "tonight Julius is having supper at home."